Grandma's Triumph
A Story of Family Unity in Overcoming Cancer presented by
Granddaughter
(Based on a true story)

Grandma's Triviedi

Jahanvi Trivedi and Aadhya Trivedi

Published by Jahanvi Trivedi, 2024.

This is a work of fiction. Similarities to real people, places, or events are entirely coincidental.

GRANDMA'S TRIUMPH

First edition. November 29, 2024.

Copyright © 2024 Jahanvi Trivedi and Aadhya Trivedi.

ISBN: 979-8230813866

Written by Jahanvi Trivedi and Aadhya Trivedi.

To all the brave souls battling cancer,

This book is dedicated to you—the fighters, the survivors, and those who have faced this journey with unwavering strength. Your resilience lights the way for others, showing that hope can flourish even in the darkest moments.

To the doctors, nurses, and caregivers who dedicate their lives to healing, your compassion and expertise make all the difference. You are the guiding hands that help transform fear into courage, and despair into hope.

To the unwavering strength of family, who stood together in love and unity during the darkest of times.

May this story of recovery inspire you all to keep pushing forward, to find joy in the small victories, and to hold on to the belief that brighter days are always ahead. Your journeys are powerful, and together, we can continue to spread hope and strength. May our journey remind others that love can conquer even the toughest battles!

Preface

In every family, there are stories that become legends, passed down through generations. This is one such story—told through the eyes of a loving granddaughter who witnessed her grandmother's extraordinary battle against cancer.

Ganga, the grandmother, is a woman of incredible grace and strength. Her journey through the challenges of cancer was both heart-wrenching and awe-inspiring. Her granddaughter had the privilege of watching her navigate this formidable fight with unwavering courage and a spirit that never faltered.

This story is not just about the medical struggle but about the profound impact of family. It was through the collective love, support, and resilience of the family that the grandma found the strength to persevere. Family's shared moments of hope, the quiet encouragements, and the heartfelt connections formed the bedrock of her fight.

As you delve into this narrative, you will discover not just a tale of illness and recovery but a celebration of the human spirit and the unbreakable bonds of family. The grandmother's story is a testament to the power of love, the importance of support, and the incredible strength that can emerge from even the toughest of battles.

May this story inspire you to cherish the ones you love, find hope in the face of adversity, and recognize the profound difference that family and perseverance can make in any struggle.

Acknowledgment

I, Jahanvi Trivedi, extend my heartfelt gratitude to the omnipotent forces of life.

I am immensely thankful for the support of our loved ones, relatives, and friends who have been with us throughout my beloved mother's health recovery journey.

A special thanks to my mother, Manjula Modha for sharing her authentic experiences of recovery from cancer and inspiring us all. I also express my deep appreciation to my father, Bharat Modha, the eternal source of energy and inspiration. His presence has made this journey and our story complete. I am grateful to my brother Sanjay Modha, Sister in law Sheetal Modha, nephew Kush Modha, and husband Sandeep Trivedi for their unwavering support during Manjula's difficult times. I honor my late elders, Mr. Janakrai Trivedi and Mrs. Jaiwanti Trivedi, for their enduring blessings and love.

A heartfelt acknowledgment goes to Kush Modha for his incredible design of the book cover.

I am also deeply grateful to my daughter, Aadhya Trivedi, for crafting the beautiful plot of this story.

Lastly, thank you to our dear friends for being our inspiration and unwavering supporters.

Contents

Chapters:

Disclaimer

This story is intended for motivational purposes and maintenance of positive attitude during the tough times.

The story is not a substitute for professional medical advice. The experiences and strategies described are based on the personal journey of the individual featured and may not reflect universal outcomes. The treatments and ideas presented in the story may not be suitable for everyone and should not be considered as a one-size-fits-all solution. Each person's situation is unique, and it is essential to seek guidance from qualified healthcare professionals.

Please consult with healthcare professionals for personalized medical advice and treatment options tailored to your specific needs.

Chapter 1 "Swallow the Weakness"
In shadows cast, your hearts unite,
Together strong, you face the fight.
With love as armor, hope as light,
Each day a step, through darkest night.
Hold hands and share the laughter's glow,
For in your strength, new courage grows.
With every breath, remember this:
Love conquers all; together, you'll rise from the abyss.

The grandma's room was dimly lit, but her spirit shone brighter than any light I had ever seen. As she blessed and wished me "Happy Birthday" on the midnight hour of my birthday May 1, 2024, I couldn't avoid the feeling that we were all warriors in this fight against cancer, united like an unbreakable chain. With each round of treatment, it wasn't just her body battling the illness—it was our entire family, armed with love, laughter, and an unwavering belief that hope could conquer even the darkest moments. "Together, we're unstoppable," she whispered, her eyes glistening with determination. Little did I know, her journey would transform us all, revealing the true power of love in the face of adversity.

The battle starts.....

December 16, 2022. It was my grandma's birthday. Me, Abhimanyu, Mom and Dad had gone to my maternal grandmother Ganga's house to take blessings. Grandma and I are each other's best buddies. She has shared most of her life experiences with me.

"A thirty-six year old Ganga would have never believed something like this to happen." said Ganga grandma to me, now turning 72 years young. She was showing me all her young age photographs while telling me stories about her life as a teacher. The thing her younger version could not believe was in fact about a cheater. She was very fond of her one student Rohan- a smart kid who got straight A's in all the subjects, a social butterfly, and moreover, liked by all. She came across his picture and started telling me the incident.

Once while invigilating an exam, she found Rohan being super anxious about something- maybe exam stress? She came up to him and asked what was wrong but Rohan just faked a smile and buried his head into his paper. It was after the exam that she found out Rohan was worried about whether or not to help a friend with a question. Ganga was relieved to know that Rohan had not cheated in his exam, but then years after she had retired, she found out Rohan was a cheater and had asked another friend to help him with a question. She was always concerned about her children's values. She not only wanted to teach bookish knowledge but also moral values. This incident had really broken her heart.

She was so disappointed that day, and even while telling this to me now, she had an apathetic look on her face.

"Forget about the people who hurt you, grandmother, and tell me more about the fun stuff!" I told Ganga to divert her mind while lifting up another picture. My grandma and I often share our experiences with one another. I also love telling stories about my school and friends, to her.

I am, by the way, Vandana, a 13 year old daughter of Ganga Joshi's daughter, Surbhi. I stay with my family in Mumbai, India. My mother Surbhi acquired a job at a higher post when I was about four years old, but since her office was rather far from our house, she would drop my 10 year old brother Abhimanyu and me off at my grandparents' place. It was only a mile from our residence to their residence. Since 10 years, I've been pretty close to them.

My grandma was a school teacher in her young days. She has served the children for almost 30+ years. She has not only imparted good education in children but also gave them good values of life. Such a humble job!

"Oh my goodness, you haven't eaten anything yet! Please wait while I grab you some strawberries that we have. Abhimanyu go get some..."

Ganga was chatting about food as usual. Every time my mom and I visit her home, it's customary for her to watch us masticating something from her kitchen. It seems that we cannot leave her house without eating. Strawberries would have been fine for now, but if it had been up to her, she would have given us a whole refrigerator full of food.

"Why aren't you eating anything?" my mother asked Ganga. "Surbhi, my darling, my stomach always gets full when I see you kids eat." stated Ganga sweetly.

"Surbhi let her be." My mother's brother Sameer remarked, "You know her character, she will not eat until you finish eating."

Ganga's actions would constantly bother him too much, and he would prefer it if she were more sensible. According to Sameer uncle's wife, Shanaya, the previous day Ganga had lost her balance due to the simple statement, "I get full while watching you eat," as she had abruptly fallen backwards while seated on a couch. This was excessive.

"Mother in law, I've noticed that you're fainting a lot these days. I believe that a person's desire for energy cannot be satisfied by simply watching other people eat." stated Shanaya.

"Repeated fainting isn't quite normal, mother." Sameer continued. "I believe we ought to go see a doctor so they can treat you."

When Ganga heard this, she defended her decision to forego going to the doctor right away, saying, "Oh no need! I'm doing fine. This is an unpredictable age. It's quite acceptable to..."

"You are in your early seventies. This age group is rather unpredictable. Anything is possible. No matter how many justifications you offer, you ARE going to the doctor, early tomorrow morning. Its final." firmly exclaimed Sameer. When dawn came, everyone prepared to head to the infirmary.

"I don't want to go, Sameer. It doesn't feel right. Please let's return home. Why do we have to travel to another town when we could attend the clinic that is only two blocks away?" Ganga asked her son all the time, but Sameer never answered.

Ganga started coming up with more and more plausible justifications during the car ride, but Sameer would not listen to her. But then he finally gave up.

"Mom, tell me why you're against visiting the doctor. If your concerns are about them being let loose with their sniffer dogs or giving you unnecessary injections, they won't do either."

Ganga bowed her head, acknowledging her error. Her son only desired what was best for her. In actuality, Ganga was concerned about being admitted to a sanatorium in the event that a major ailment was discovered. At last, she gave in and made the decision to visit the hospital. After one or two hours, the physician finished his examination and shared his diagnosis.

"Mr. Joshi, there's no need for concern; it appears to be a mild case of a common virus. This virus causes colds, coughs, appetite loss, and odor loss. Despite its appearance, it is not the coronavirus. It takes her a few days to heal." The doctor inquired, "She has taken the senior citizen booster vaccination dose, right?" to which Sameer responded in the affirmation. "Then you should give her these prescriptions. These are available for purchase in the ground floor pharmacy."

It was funny to watch Uncle Sameer talk to the doctor in that way. Sameer uncle was nodding his head like a submissive child while the doctor spoke and gave instructions. On the other side, my grandfather Shankar was persuading my grandma Ganga, who refused to comply with everything the doctor suggested since she didn't want to take medication.

"Also, you need to take a device called a 'nebulizer'. It is basically a small device that can turn liquid medicine into mist to be inhaled easily. It will ease your discomfort and aid in relieving the stiffened cough in your lungs. You can buy that from the pharmacy as well." completed the doctor.

Sameer uncle purchased every item needed for Ganga's care. Ganga was following her husband, her son, and the physicians' instructions but with reluctance.

"Why is this stupid nebulizer necessary? Ginger tea can be used to cure a common cold. Would you mind making me some ginger tea, Shanaya, please?" Ganga stated, refusing to take her medication.

"Please, you don't need any tea. Remember to keep in mind of your diabetes too, mother. Tea is off limits to you. Please finish the nebulizer's recommended dosage for the day. After all, it's only in your best interest." interrupted Sameer.

These tantrums continued for a week, but somehow everyone was able to get her to finish her medication. The cold and cough went away.

Perhaps Grandma is doing better now, I thought to myself after a month had passed. We had gathered at their home once again for the New Year party. It's truly remarkable how Ganga still exudes such energy at her age! This time she herself made tasty food for all of us. Hot puris and Green vegetables are grandma's specialty. While Shanaya aunty is expert in making gulab jamuns and fried fritters especially for me as she knows most of my favorite dishes. Looking at the cheerful faces of all elders, I started imagining for a small celebration. I was eagerly waiting to request elders to plan a small picnic at the end of the New Year vacation in my little brain. Yet somehow I was worried and scared to ask this to elders. Why? While everything was so cheerful, there was some sadness on everyone's face. We all talked and ate a lot of food at the dinner table. It took around 1 hour for us to finish our dinner. However Sameer uncle noticed that grandma is still eating. Her tiring expressions while swallowing the food were clearly visible.

"Mother, what is going on with you? Are you okay? Besides this, you also look little weak?" Sameer said in a worried manner.

"Son, I have no idea. I'm finding it difficult to swallow." Ganga remarked, "It feels like there's a lump in the way of my bolus."

"Mother-in-law, I've noticed that you're not eating properly your food. You must consume the food despite its resistance; else, you will become weaker every day!" said Shanaya.

"Oh Shanaya, she's already become weak." said Shankar. "She can't even sit for too long." he continued as Ganga moved to go to her bedroom. He sarcastically whispered to Shanaya, "Look now she won't even remember to drink water. Oh, and speaking of remembering, she's basically forgetting everything these days. She brought me a rosemary plant out of the blue earlier today, and she forgot about it when I asked why! She's becoming really silly."

"Grandpa, a few days ago, grandmother had handed my mother and me ten thousand bucks for no apparent reason. Despite the fact that it was not anyone's birthday, celebration, or account, she gave my mother the money forcefully." I stated. Deep inside I was happy to receive this money but when I came to know about grandma's forgetfulness, I also got worried.

Everyone was quite concerned after that. Shankar expressed alarm, saying, "This weakness, this forgetfulness, this trouble in swallowing, doesn't seem right."

Everyone agreed to it and decided to approach the doctor again next day without Ganga's knowledge.

"Imagine if she could try to *swallow the weakness*!" commented Shanaya trying to lighten everybody's mood.

Chapter 2 Nothing to worry:

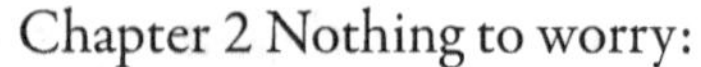

"I'm not interested in going! We went recently, right? Why should I visit the doctor every day? I don't need to visit the hospital frequently. I am not a chronic patient. Why even is there trouble if my common cold has been already cured?" Ganga refused to go to the doctor because she was obstinate.

"Please, mom, no more excuses. You have to know that I am worried about your health. Why do you fear visiting the doctor so much? They won't give you unnecessary injections, as I already stated," explained Sameer.

He was getting irritated because Ganga was repeating what she had done before. After numerous small-talk disputes, they eventually arrived at the physicians.

"You had been here before too, didn't you?" asked the physician.

"Yes."

"What happened? Did the cold persist or what?"

"No, the chill has passed. Rather, she is experiencing difficulty with food swallowing. Doctor, I'm worried. Please lend a hand with it." Then Sameer went on to describe whatever Ganga was going through.

"To me, that seems like a typical instance of GERD. Be at ease. The symptoms..."

"I'm sorry to interrupt, but what is GERD?"

"Oh. It is basically gastro esophageal reflux disease. A digestive disease in which stomach acid or bile irritates the food pipe lining and may cause a burning sensation or trouble in swallowing. The illness is moderate. I'll evaluate her first, and if GERD is present, I'll outline the necessary treatment.

Ganga was examined by the doctor, who also asked a million questions. "What sort of cuisine do you consume?

"Normal routine food like chapatti and sabzi, daal and rice. Doctor, nothing to worry I am alright." Said Ganga.

"Ok, what did you eat today?"

"Simple dishes. Chapati, potato sabzi and khichdi. Doctor, nothing to worry I am alright." said Ganga.

"Have you ever experienced a similar disease in the past?"

"No Doctor. Nothing to worry...."

"Yes, yes, I know you're alright," the doctor said, interrupting Ganga with a smile. He must have been thinking, 'What kind of patient is this? Instead of me reassuring her, she's the one reassuring me!' Then he finally said, "These are a few tests that I'm prescribing. We can't presume whether this is GERD or not yet but please get the tests finished and bring the reports to me. Come back on Tuesday, at five in the evening." At the end of the prescriptions for various tests he wrote "Nothing to worry" with a smiling emoji.

Sameer made Ganga do half of the tests that day itself and the rest the next day. Three days later, all the reports came in. Sameer took only the blood reports to show, as instructed by the doctor.

"Well, Ganga-ji, you really should look after yourself. There is no GERD but still Your reports don't really appeal to me." The doctor said, "Mr. Sameer, please look over the reports while I put together a diet plan for her."

While reviewing the results, Sameer deduced that Ganga may have certain vitamin deficiencies; however he was unsure about this. He observed the physician preparing a lengthy diet chart with stringent diabetes management for Ganga.

"Doctor, I can see my mother has some vitamin deficiency, but can you please elaborate on it?"

"Yes certainly. Your mother has numerous vitamin and nutrient deficits, some minor, some severe. Minor shortages include hemoglobin, iron, and ascorbic acid (vitamin C). These can be treated with regular vitamin supplements, but the big ones necessitate a healthy diet and extra care."

"Doctor you are scaring us!"

"There's no reason to get scared; the eating plan isn't that restrictive. The majority of the food is in your typical meal."

"So the significant flaws aren't that bad?"

"Cobalamin, retinol, vitamin B12, and vitamin A are the deficits. These are present in green vegetables, dairy products, and carrots, among other foods. They are not extreme, so chill." ended the doctor with a gawky laughter.

There was a brief pause and awkward silence before the doctor added, "Follow this eating plan and take the vitamins for about two months, then return on the ides of May. Hopefully, all of the issues will be addressed by then."

Ganga could not find any clue out of this conversation. What she understood until now was that she needs to eat a lot of food which is called a balanced diet.

After leaving the hospital, Sameer gave Ganga a side eye, as if to confront her carelessness in eating well. Even Shankar was disappointed with her. They scolded her for her irresponsibility. "So deficiencies it is then..." they said jointly.

Chapter 3 Its vacation time!

Ganga adhered strictly to her supplement dosage and food plan. But one day when I had visited her, we being besties or best friends, she had shared with me her difficulties in swallowing those pills and eating her unfavorite vegetables. I could relate her situation with mine as I have many a times eaten certain unappetizing food my mother had prepared when I had fallen sick. And I can't describe how boring it is to fall sick and eat not so tasty food. What can I do in this? My childish brain started to find some idea of relieving my grandma from this boredom. Then suddenly an idea struck my mind.

I asked her if she would like to eat icecream as cough and cold had been cured by now. She merrily nodded her head. I placed an online order from my mobile app and chose the option of cash on delivery. But now I got nervous to ask any one in her house to pay for the icecream. What will happen if grandpa will reject the order? What if Sameer uncle scolds me for ordering this icecream as grandma's entire diet was strictly prepared as per her diet chart. My heart beats started increasing as the estimated delivery time was decreasing minute by minute. Then the doorbell rang. My grandpa opened the door. Yes, I guessed right. It was icecream delivery man holding a BIG family pack of the strawberry icecream. Grandpa normally collected the icecream and paid for it. His facial expressions remained completely neutral, as if nothing unusual had occurred. Meanwhile, my mouth was agape, and my jaw dropped in astonishment at Grandpa's lack of reaction.

"What's the matter? Don't be surprised," he said with a smile. "I ordered this ice cream for you and Grandma. I noticed you two talking about ice cream and saw that you'd ordered just a small pack for her on your app. So, I decided to upgrade it to a big family pack. Don't worry—Grandma can enjoy ice cream at intervals, once a week or so. I am bringing this icecream in bowl, now you both the kids, i.e. you and your grandma, enjoy this icecream. This ice cream is a reward for the care and love you've shown to your grandma."

Our little ice cream party began, and before we knew it, the entire family pack was devoured by just the two of us. I'm certain my brother Abhi will be upset when he hears about this, but it's okay. I'm confident that Grandpa will make sure he gets his own ice cream too.

After a few days of strict diet with some small episodes of icecream parties, grandma was becoming livelier.

The Ides of May were still far off, so Ganga decided to take her annual vacation to her hometown of Porbandar, Gujarat. Porbandar, a small town in southern Gujarat, holds great historical significance as the birthplace of Mahatma Gandhi, our revered father of the nation. Since my Mom shared this information with me, I have felt a deep sense of pride in our connection to this city. As for Grandma and Grandpa, they have their own siblings living there and have spent a significant part of their lives in Porbandar—from their birth and schooling to their careers. Even my Mom and Sameer uncle grew up there during their school years. My Mom often reminisces about her hometown, sharing vivid stories of her school days, friends, and childhood games in the rain and with clay. Her tales never fail to captivate me and make me marvel at how life once seemed so simple and joyful, without the distractions of modern technology.

And what do I say about grandpa and grandma. They feel like coming home whenever they visit Porbandar. Their hometown trip was their me-time where they can enjoy a full life with siblings, friends, nostalgic first home which they had built with their first earnings. I and Abhi have also been in that home which is the coziest place in the world. We can't compare hometown and that home stay with any other trip whether national or international, whether in 3 star or 5 star hotel. The home is built in an old style. It has a ground floor with our own terrace. And the compound of the home is amazing. Even I and Abhi have lots of our sweet moments there. It is rightly said that home is where family not only stays but lives. My grandpa and grandma have their memories even with their own parents who are no more. The home is not just a building but a beautiful story in itself. When asked my mom and Sameer uncle, why they left their hometown, they had only one answer, that is because of their future. Then I understood how difficult it would have been for grandma and grandpa to leave all their beloveds and their own home for the future of their children. All respect to their sacrifices.

On the day of the journey, I could see the pure joy on my grandma's and grandpa's faces, as if they were children again. If they had the energy, they would have leaped with excitement! Sameer Uncle drove them to the Panvel railway station, where they were set to catch a direct train to Porbandar.

Sameer Uncle dropped them off at the railway station and had to leave for work. As the platform was long and the spot where their coach would arrive was quite a distance away, so Grandma and Grandpa began to walk. Unfortunately, Grandma's health issues soon became apparent, and she struggled with the distance. Feeling exhausted and unsteady, she collapsed on the platform just as the train arrived. However, catching this train was crucial since the tickets had been booked three months in advance and reservations would be lost if they missed it.

Thanks to the assistance of the public and the police, immediate help was provided. The police ensured that their luggage was loaded onto the train, while several people helped Grandma board the train as well. The entire 21-hour train journey was filled with tension and prayers, hoping for no further issues.

After they reached Porbandar, all the relatives started pouring into the house asking about their well-being. When grandpa narrated this entire episode on phone to us, Mom and Sameer Uncle got extremely scared.

"You need to immediately return to Mumbai, Daddy. We can't afford to keep you both all by yourself there and play with your health." Sameer uncle urged Grandpa. However, his words had little effect. Grandpa and grandma were determined to stay there. Not only stay there but also they planned of celebrating with relatives the Purushottam month. They wanted to invite all 90-100 relatives for lunch. Now that was a truly courageous step. I had heard Sameer uncle and mom discussing about this bold step of their parents. I remembered a time when I refused to go to school because of a slight fever, throwing a tantrum despite my parents' patient explanations. They grew exhausted trying to convince me that my fever was minor, but my teenage stubbornness only made it seem worse. Eventually, my parents gave up trying to persuade me to go. Looking back, I realize that if I had attended school that day, I might have felt proud of my decision. It's fascinating how these seemingly small events play a significant role in shaping our personalities, isn't it?

Grandpa organized the entire lunch celebration while also managing Grandma's health. They hosted the event for all their relatives in

Porbandar. Mom kept questioning the necessity of the gathering, but Grandma was steadfast in her plans. Perhaps this is how the elderly find joy—by gathering with family, seeing their loved ones, and finding happiness in the act of hosting and feeding them.

'We're so happy here. Are you happy now?' Grandpa asked Sameer uncle and Mom during a video call that evening, after recounting the entire event and how much they had enjoyed organizing and hosting it. 'Yes, we agree,' Mom replied with a smile. 'You two are truly one-of-a-kind parents.'

Chapter 4 Grandma's return home: Hernia detection

Seeing Grandma and Grandpa so happy, my family in Mumbai began planning a long pending international trip to Dubai. Though Grandpa and Grandma never accompany us to any of such trips, we are okay with the arrangement. They have their own share of happiness at hometown with relatives while we Six i.e. Sameer uncle, Shanaya aunty, Mom, Dad, me and Abhi enjoy national and international trips. Abhi and I were thrilled at the prospect. Mom, Dad, Sameer uncle, and Shanaya Aunty were busy arranging our visas, tickets, and Dubai currency. This would be our first international trip, and we could hardly contain our excitement. The moment we received our visas and tickets was unforgettable, especially when I got the first stamp in my passport. Until, now I was aware of only one use of passport ie. Identity and address proof. Now I came to know this other use as well. The trip was scheduled in late October 2023.

Then came the big news of my grandpa and grandma arriving back home in Mumbai. It was September 2023, and I was overjoyed at the prospect of receiving local sweets and snacks from Porbandar, especially the rare Khajli, which is seldom found in Mumbai. I could hardly wait to taste those treats and hear all about their trip.

However, my excitement couldn't last long. Their return was marred by distressing news: just a day before boarding the train, Grandma's health had deteriorated in Porbandar. She had collapsed at home, which was a harsh blow. I couldn't help but wonder why Grandma was facing so many health challenges. The situation seemed so unfair and overwhelming. Thankfully, my other uncles and aunts in Porbandar stepped in to help, providing care and support during this critical time. There was even a moment when Grandpa thought about postponing the journey back to Mumbai. However, the doctors administered temporary treatment and advised Grandma to get further checkups once they arrived in Mumbai. Despite everything and amidst all this chaos, Grandpa still managed to bring my favorite snacks and sweets. What kind of heart do grandparents have? Even while facing their own challenges, they remembered what their grandchildren love. I can't help but wonder if I'll have the same kind of selflessness and thoughtfulness when I grow older. For now, I've resolved to prioritize Grandma's health and accept that our Dubai trip might need to be canceled.

Sameer uncle took Grandma to the doctor once again. Is it true that a once-sick patient always seems to be a patient? Grandma has always told me she doesn't like being ill. She's so mentally strong that I've never heard her complain about even a minor headache. She rarely takes a break from her work. Mom often described Grandma as the family's darling. As the eldest sibling, she took on the responsibility of finding suitable life partners for all her brothers and sisters, managing their weddings with grace. She is equally dear to her in laws. As the only daughter in law, she took utmost care of her mother-in-law. I have often heard the great words from my grandpa about her caring and sacrificing nature towards people. Being a school teacher, she is a strong advocate for education. She continually offers me guidance and advice about my own studies, reflecting her lifelong passion for learning.

Now, I see her taking medication constantly and speaking very little. A noticeable sadness has settled on her face. I find myself praying, "Oh God, please help my grandma overcome her suffering." This time, the doctor discovered that she is suffering from an intestinal hernia, where a part of the large intestine protrudes near the navel. This condition prevents food from moving through the digestive system properly, leading to loss of appetite and persistent constipation. The doctor has recommended that she undergo surgery as soon as possible.

This was a time of great dilemma. "We are not going to Dubai," Sameer uncle and Dad announced, a decision we had all been already anticipating. I noticed a tear slide down Sameer uncle's cheek, while Mom wept quietly. It was clear that both of them were deeply concerned about their mother. Abhi and I had already accepted the elders' decision. This was not the time for tantrums but for showing our support.

Soon, a new debate arose. Grandpa, as usual, was reluctant to cancel the trip stating his great capacity as a caretaker of his wife alone. Then one after another, the elders—Mom, Sameer uncle, Dad, and Shanaya Aunty—discussed how to manage the situation, with each one offering to stay behind with Grandpa while the rest of us can go on the trip. However, it became clear that Abhi's and my trip would be canceled. Personally, we also felt it was important not to leave Grandpa and Grandma in their current condition. As a child, I hoped to contribute by doing my best to cheer them up.

The elders decided to schedule Grandma's surgery for the end of September 2023. She was hospitalized for a week, and Mom and I visited her every day. On the first day after the operation, Grandma was unable to move and was instructed to stay in bed without any movement. She had two tubes connected to her: one for glucose and one for urine. The hospital environment felt overwhelmingly somber, with patients and their families all enveloped in deep grief. What a sad place, I thought.

"Hey Vandana, did you watch that movie *Barbie*?" Grandpa suddenly asked, jolting me from my thoughts. I was taken aback. How could Grandpa be so unexpectedly cool? Had he lost his mind, or had God granted him some kind of superpower?

"No, but Mom has promised to take me to see it," I replied. I knew Grandpa would likely scold Mom for this.

"Come on, Surbhi, you should take her to the movie," Grandpa said, practically issuing an order.

"Yes, I'll take her as soon as Mom gets home. Don't worry," Mom responded, making a face that clearly showed her discomfort.

The next day, when we visited Grandma, her glucose tube had been removed, and she was now able to sit up and eat properly. That evening, her urine tube was also taken out. On the third day, as Mom and I were preparing to visit Grandma, her phone rang. Annoyed by the interruption, Mom answered, expecting it to be a telemarketer she would promptly hang up on. To her surprise, it was Grandpa calling.

"Hello," she answered. "Yes, okay, oh, alright." I was deeply worried, fearing that there might be more complications with Grandma's health. What could have happened? Had the doctors extended her hospital stay?

After a lengthy conversation, Mom finally hung up the phone and shared the good news: Grandma was coming home. The doctors had discharged her after just three days instead of the anticipated week. It was a delightful surprise, especially since we hadn't had any pleasant news in nearly nine months. When Grandma returned from the hospital, it felt like celebrating Diwali before the actual festival. We all rejoiced with an ice cream party, knowing how much we kids love it! Grandma was recovering and slowly improving. Although she couldn't eat normally, her digestive process had significantly improved. Despite this, grandma and grandpa encouraged us to proceed with our Dubai trip.

What a trip it was—my first international adventure! I learned so much from the experience. For starters, I discovered what it's like to wake up at 2 a.m. I took on the task of waking up Mom and Dad, a role typically reversed for school and exams. However, when it comes to picnics or trips, I proudly handle the wake-up calls. We were ready in two hours and caught a cab to the airport with Sameer uncle and Shanaya aunty at 4 a.m. After completing all the visa checks and luggage check-ins, we boarded our flight at around 9:30 a.m. from Mumbai. The flight took about three hours, and we landed in Dubai at 11 a.m.! It was a jet lag experience, as Dubai is 1.5 hours behind Indian Standard Time. Though I had heard about jet lag before, this was my first time experiencing it. Now I can proudly tell my friends that I'm an experienced international traveler and I know exactly what jet lag feels like!

We stayed at a hotel and explored many wonderful places in Dubai, from the desert to a scenic cruise, and had a blast throughout the trip. Throughout our travels, Grandpa frequently called to get updates, and both he and Grandma seemed to enjoy our stories as if they were right there with us. As our return approached, I found it hard to let go of the excitement, but I reminded myself that every enjoyable experience eventually leads to the next one.

That mindset helped me adjust. At the Dubai airport on our way back, Mom and Dad planned to host a Navratri bhoj for all my friends just two days later. I was thrilled—one more fun event to look forward to! Throughout the Dubai trip and in the time that followed, we didn't think much about Grandma's health as Grandpa didn't let us think about it. He attended to all her needs whole heartedly.

After returning from Dubai, we were busy preparing for the Navratri Bhoj. I quickly made a guest list of girls to be invited, while Mom and Dad planned the menu, which would include Puri, Chhole, Pulav, Kheer, and salad—delicious and mouthwatering! Mom and Dad preferred to cook everything themselves for this event. This yearly event was something Grandma and Grandpa always attended wholeheartedly, often bringing their homemade Dhokla for the girls. Navratri, a celebration of the triumph of Nav Durga over evil, is a time when it's considered auspicious to worship and feed young girls and offer them gifts. I had attended similar bhojans at other houses and received my favorite gifts, adding to the festive spirit.

This time, however, things were different. We celebrated Navratri Bhoj without my grandparents, as they were unable to leave their home. The menu was prepared, but sadly, there was no Dhokla. The event was filled with enthusiasm, yet tinged with sadness. Grandma was suffering from severe weakness, and Grandpa stayed behind to care for her. Mom had packed up the delicious dishes for them, but the next day we learned that Grandma hadn't been able to taste any of the food.

My young mind was troubled, trying to understand why Grandma couldn't eat properly even after her operation. Deep inside I was constantly praying to goddess Navdurga to remove all the obstacles from my grandma's life. Just like Navdurga killed the demons and succeeded in saving the human kind, I prayed her for killing all bad virus or bacteria in grandma's body and save her.

Once again, Sameer uncle decided to take Grandma to the doctor. This time, the doctor confirmed that her hernia operation was successful, which was a relief. However, he recommended that she see a gastroenterologist for further evaluation. A gastroenterologist is a specialist in gastrointestinal diseases. They focus on diagnosing and treating conditions affecting the digestive system, including the esophagus, stomach, and intestines, as well as the biliary organs such as the liver, bile ducts, pancreas, and gallbladder. This step was essential to ensure comprehensive care and address any remaining health concerns.

Chapter 5 Cancer- our biggest enemy

The gastroenterologists recommended an angiography of the esophagus, or food pipe.

"What is Angiography? And why mom has to go through it? Is it painful? Is it okay at this age of her to go through this test? Sameer uncle asked all the questions at once. "Have patience, Sameer. There is nothing to worry. It is an X-ray procedure that examines blood vessels in the body. It's performed by an interventional radiologist who injects a special dye into your blood vessels, called a contrast agent, to highlight them. The X-ray images created during the procedure are called angiograms. We will give local anesthesia so that your mom will not feel any pain of the procedure however she will remain awake during the procedure." explained the doctor.

"Son, whatever it turns out to be, I'm ready. Don't worry," Grandma told Sameer Uncle. He was taken aback, as just the few months before, she had been reluctant to use a nebulizer, yet today she was prepared for the angiography. The shift in her attitude was striking! Usually, Grandma avoids acknowledging minor health issues, preferring to tough it out rather than burden her family. However, this time, she must have sensed something more serious was wrong inside her body and needed immediate attention. It was a moment for her to be strong rather than succumb to weakness.

When grandma was taken for the procedure, the doctor was surprised to find that the tool could only be inserted a few inches into the esophagus. It became evident that something was obstructing the passage, which had not been anticipated. This was the first time the doctor and our family learned about a tumor developing inside the esophagus. The discovery was unsettling and raised immediate concerns. The doctor took a tissue sample from the tumor and sent it to the laboratory for testing. I watched as all my elders—Grandpa, Sameer uncle and Shanaya Aunty, Mom and Dad, and Abhi—grew increasingly concerned about what the tumor might be. We anxiously awaited the results.

It was the time of Diwali, when Abhi and I typically receive our annual cash gifts from Grandpa and Grandma. These gifts are a cherished blessing from our elders, tokens of their love that always light up our celebrations. Diwali is celebrated across India to mark the return of Lord Rama to Ayodhya after his victory over the demon king Ravana. However, my young mind was preoccupied with concern for my own 'Ram'—Grandma—and when she would return to full health. Every flickering diya and burst of firecracker seemed to echo my worry, a stark reminder of her absence. The laughter and festivity around us felt hollow as we received the reports and began to apply our limited knowledge in an attempt to understand them. Each word in those documents seemed to weigh heavy on our hearts, casting a shadow over the festival that was otherwise meant to be filled with joy.

"What is it?" Grandpa asked me, jolting me from my deep thoughts. I drew on my basic school knowledge of biology and ventured an interpretation.

"This might be a cancerous tumor, but it seems to be at a very early stage—maybe stage 0 or 1," I said hesitantly.

"Shut up. You're not a doctor," my mom snapped, her voice tinged with disbelief. It was the first time I found myself struggling to accept the reality, so I chose not to press the matter further. Normally, I would have insisted on my understanding of science, especially since Mom's knowledge was somewhat lacking as a commerce student. Sameer Uncle and Shanaya Aunty were also trying to decipher the reports, mirroring my own uncertainties. Grandpa, meanwhile, looked increasingly anxious.

Grandma was resting peacefully in her room, unaware of the arrival of the report. The adults were debating whether, if the doctor confirmed a cancer diagnosis, they should tell grandma. It was at this moment that my Grandpa, with unwavering resolve, declared that grandma was strong enough to handle the truth about her condition and the necessary treatment. "Let's not hide anything from her," he insisted. "She is incredibly strong. Whether facing financial hardships, health crises, or career struggles of family members, she has always triumphed over every challenge. I am deeply proud of her courage and am committed to standing by her through this toughest journey of our lives." His words conveyed a sense of unshakable strength, as if he were not just a man but a steadfast mountain, unwavering and resolute before us. Why not, after all, he and grandma had shared over 50 years together; their bond was deep and resilient enough to face this challenge jointly. The true challenge of grandma and our family started now. The physical weakness, partial memory loss, hernia and diminished logical thinking were merely symptoms of this larger issue.

The next day, Sameer uncle took the report to the doctor, who confirmed that the cancer was at an early stage, below stage one. Relief mingled with anxiety as we clung to the hope that it was not too late. The doctor recommended a PET scan to precisely determine the size and extent of the tumor. PET stands for Positron Emission Tomography. A PET scan is a type of imaging test that uses a radioactive substance to create pictures of the body and show how organs and tissues are functioning. The scan would give us a clearer picture, but the uncertainty was nerve-wracking. He ruled out surgery due to two main factors: Grandma's age and the tumor's location within the esophagus i.e. food pipe which is a muscular tube that moves food from mouth to stomach.

The doctor's words were heavy as he outlined the proposed treatment plan, which involved a combination of chemotherapy and radiation. "Ganga will need 28 to 30 sessions of radiation and 6 chemotherapy treatments over the next 6 weeks. But she will not require any hospitalization. Sameer, you will have to bring her to the hospital for the radiation and chemo sessions for next 6 weeks." he said, his voice steady but somber. "Each session will be a battle, a testament to her strength."

Sameer uncle's voice trembled as he asked, "How will we manage this? Will she be able to handle it?"

The doctor nodded, acknowledging the gravity of his concern. "It will be tough, no doubt. The treatment is grueling and will test both Ganga's endurance and the patience of her family."

"Doctor, we're set to begin treatment next week. Could you please provide an estimate of the costs involved?" asked Sameer uncle.

"Of course," the doctor replied, picking up a pen and paper. He carefully detailed the expenses for each radiation session, chemotherapy, medications, and any potential extra charges for unforeseen or emergency treatments. The total estimate came to around 3 to 4 lakhs.

"Mr. Sameer, do you have mediclaim coverage for Ganga?" the doctor inquired.

"Yes, doctor. We have a family mediclaim. Even if some expenses aren't covered, I assure you I'll take care of every need for my mother," Sameer uncle responded earnestly.

The doctor was glad to see Sameer uncle's commitment towards his mom.

"Sameer, we have a Fixed Deposit set aside for emergencies like this. We can manage the expenses," Grandpa said, holding his hand reassuringly.

"No, Father. Let me handle this. I've set aside a portion of my income for situations like these. If I can afford an international trip for my family, I can certainly save for emergencies," Sameer replied confidently.

"God bless you, my son," Grandpa said, his eyes shining with pride. My little brain thought, I could grow up to be just like Sameer uncle—wise, kind, and loving."

"Anyway, having enough money doesn't mean we shouldn't seek a second opinion, right, son?" Grandpa suggested.

"Of course, Dad. I've scheduled an appointment at another hospital tomorrow. It may be less well-known, but it will definitely help us weigh our options and find the best treatment," Sameer replied.

The next day, Sameer presented the same reports to the second hospital, and the second doctor confirmed everything the first doctor had said. After comparing the various options of hospital facilities, distance of hospitals from home, and convenience of taking Grandma every day to the hospital, two best hospitals were selected. Grandpa and Sameer uncle carefully considered factors such as the expertise of the medical staff, the availability of specialized treatments, and the overall patient experience. One for radiation sessions and one for chemotherapy.

The decision was made. Grandpa glanced at the family, their faces a mix of fear and determination. "We'll do whatever it takes," he said, trying to steady his own trembling voice. "We have to stay strong for her."

Sameer uncle took a deep breath, his eyes filled with resolve. "We're in this together," he affirmed. "We'll support her through every step."

We braced ourselves for the difficult journey ahead, knowing it would challenge every ounce of our resolve.

As planned, grandma was fully informed about her condition and the treatment ahead. She mentally prepared herself, but the true intensity of the chemotherapy and radiation remained a daunting unknown. She reached out to a few relatives who had undergone similar treatments, seeking some understanding of what lay ahead. Despite this, a heavy darkness loomed over all of us, casting a shadow over our lives.

My young mind struggled to process the emotional weight of the situation. What would the future hold? Would grandma ever return to her former health? Would she lose her hair or suffer significant weight loss from the treatment? The questions swirled in my mind, unanswered and unsettling.

With my limited knowledge of human anatomy and the digestive system from my biology classes, I understood that the cancer was affecting grandma's esophagus, making it difficult for her to swallow food. The gravity of her condition was evident, but Mom and Dad, Sameer uncle and Shanaya Aunty, and grandpa were all silent. The conversation avoided the long and arduous process of treatment and its side effects, perhaps to shield grandma from the harsher realities and maintain a semblance of hope and normalcy.

Now was the time to act. There would be no more discussions, no more comforting words—only action. The journey ahead was long and arduous, but this was when our family's strength would be truly tested. Each of us made a vow to support one another and contribute in every way we could. Abhi and I took on the task of lifting everyone's spirits with our cheerful and playful chatter, determined to bring a smile to our elders' faces amidst the challenges.

Soon, Ganga's radiation sessions were set to begin. The treatment involved using a laser to target the external area where the cancerous tumor had developed. To facilitate this, the doctor ordered a specially designed jacket for her, with an opening precisely aligned with the location of the tumor. They also marked the spot with a cross for accuracy. The treatment plan was structured to include 5 radiation sessions each week, along with one chemotherapy session, for a continuous period of 6 weeks.

The radiation and chemotherapy began according to the PET scan report. The first week passed without any noticeable side effects, but unfortunately, there were no signs of improvement in Ganga's health. The entire family was on edge, anxiously waiting for any indication of progress after each radiation session. Despite our hopes, Ganga felt no change.

"Is there any improvement?" Sameer uncle asked after one of the sessions, his voice tinged with worry.

"Not yet," the doctor replied gently. "It's still early days. The effects take time."

Grandpa, sensing Sameer uncle's anxiety, gathered the family together. "The treatment process will take time," he said reassuringly. "We can't expect immediate results. We need to be patient."

As the second week arrived, the situation took a troubling turn. Grandma's weight began to plummet, dropping from 70 kg to 65 kg.

"Why is she losing so much weight?" Sameer uncle questioned, his voice strained.

"It's a common side effect," the doctor explained. "Her body is reacting to the treatment. It's important to stay focused on the long-term goal."

By the end of the second week, grandma's difficulty with swallowing had worsened.

"Why can't she swallow properly?" Sameer uncle asked, feeling helpless.

"It's a result of the treatment's impact on her esophagus," the doctor answered. "We're monitoring her closely and adjusting the care as needed."

Our growing concern was immeasurable, but we knew we had to stay strong and supportive as the journey continued.

Then came the special day of Ganga's birthday—December 16, 2023. To everyone's surprise, Grandma decided to celebrate it. We were all taken aback; in her 73 years, Ganga had never marked her birthday before. Why the sudden change? Was she perhaps thinking it might be her last celebration? The thought struck me with a chill. "Oh no, God, please don't let this be her last. If this is the case, I'll stop celebrating my birthdays too," I prayed fervently, my heart heavy with worry.

That day, we all gathered at grandma's home for the celebration. Delicious food had been ordered from a renowned local restaurant, and Sameer uncle had brought a beautiful cake. We sang "Happy Birthday" and began to enjoy the feast. I remember eating so much that I thought I might skip dinner and possibly the next two meals!

She seemed pleased watching us enjoy the food, but her own appetite was shockingly minimal.

"Mom, you need to eat more," Sameer uncle gently urged. "It's important for your strength."

Grandma smiled weakly but shook her head. "I'm just not hungry. You all enjoy. I'm happy seeing you."

We also observed that her weight loss was equally alarming. She had shed another 5 kg, dropping from 65 kg to 60 kg.

"Look at how much weight she's lost," Abhi said quietly, his face full of worry. "This can't be good."

"The side effects of the chemotherapy and radiation are really taking their toll," Dad said, his voice heavy with concern. "We need to find a way to manage this."

Despite our attempts to support her, it was clear that the treatment was having a severe impact, leaving us all deeply troubled.

Seeing her struggle, Mom began preparing homemade ice cream with minimal sugar, hoping it would help increase her weight. "She's always loved ice cream," Mom said with a hopeful smile. "Maybe this will help her gain some strength."

As I arrived with the box of homemade ice cream sent by Mom, Grandma, despite her weakness, brightened at the sight of it. Mom had entrusted me with the task of delivering the ice cream to Grandma's house quickly to prevent it from melting. Being a fellow ice cream enthusiast, I was more than happy to take on the responsibility. I was glad that Abhi was not given this task!

"Oh, this looks wonderful," Grandma said softly, managing a weak smile as she took a small spoonful. "Thank you."

"Mom, I want to be the one to deliver the ice cream to Grandma," Abhi said, his tone a bit grumpy.

"Of course, dear," Mom replied, her voice soothing. "Let Vandana handle it this week. You can take over starting next week."

Unfortunately, after a week, Grandpa noticed something troubling. "I think we need to stop giving her these frozen treats," he said with concern. "They're causing her severe coughing and cold symptoms."

Mom looked worried. "But she enjoys them so much. I thought they might help her gain some weight."

"I understand," Grandpa replied gently, "but her health is more important right now. We need to focus on what she can tolerate and what's best for her overall well-being." Despite our best efforts, Grandma's weight continued to decrease, a stark reminder of the relentless impact of the treatment.

Three weeks into the treatment, Sameer Uncle and Grandpa decided to consult the doctor about the future side effects and the progress of the tumor. The doctor reviewed the latest PET scan and informed them that the tumor had fragmented into smaller pieces, with its size drastically reduced.

He also suggested the insertion of an artificial feeding tube through the nose into the stomach.

"An artificial tube?" Grandma's voice trembled. "I've seen people with those. It's... it's unsettling."

"I know it sounds scary, Ganga ji," the doctor reassured her gently. "But it can really help you get the nutrition you need."

Grandma shook her head, her eyes wide. "The thought of having something like that... it feels so wrong. I don't know if I can do it."

The doctor paused, looking at her with compassion. "I understand this is distressing. But you've shown so much strength so far. We can take this one step at a time."

At his words, all the courage she had mustered seemed to dissolve at the mere mention of it. "I just... I don't want to lose myself in this process," she whispered.

Understanding her fear, the doctor, along with Sameer Uncle, Grandpa, and Mom, reassured her. "You won't have to endure the insertion of the feeding tube without some help," the doctor explained gently. "We'll use local anesthesia to ensure you don't feel any pain during the procedure."

Chapter 6 Silent and Flavorless

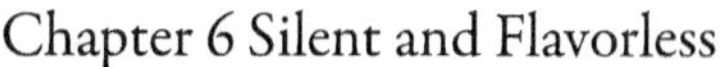

After a 4-5 day interval, the doctor inserted the feeding tube. Ganga now looked somewhat like a baby elephant with the tube in place.

"Great, now I just need a pair of big ears and I'll be all set for the circus!" she joked, trying to lighten the mood.

Her nurse chuckled, "Just don't start asking for peanuts, okay? Those might interfere with your diet!"

Ganga grinned, "Well, if I'm going to look like an elephant, I might as well eat like one!"

The nurse smiled back, "Just remember, no trumpeting in the hospital—especially during quiet hours!"

This marked the beginning of an intense phase for Grandpa. He took on the task of preparing nutritious, easily digestible foods like millets, lentils, and vegetables. The doctor also recommended protein shakes, as if Grandma was about to start a rigorous fitness regimen.

Grandpa would first prepare the food, blend it with lukewarm water in a mixer and then feed it through the tube. Sameer uncle took on the task of making the protein shakes, which were also administered through the tube. Meanwhile, my mom came up with the idea of growing wheatgrass at home to make fresh juice. She cultivated 8-9 batches of wheatgrass to ensure Grandma could have the juice every other day. Though she knew Grandma might not like the taste, it wouldn't matter since Grandma wasn't able to taste anything anyway. Given her diabetes, Grandma's tea was now sugarless, but Grandpa's nutritious feeding was hopeful for regaining her weight.

My parents also prepared a variety of other juices like carrot, beetroot, and orange to ease grandpa's workload. They began making sprouts at home to add more nutrition. Abhi and I took on the responsibility of delivering the food and drinks prepared by Mom and Dad to Grandma's home.

Despite these efforts, Grandma's lack of taste was profound. She couldn't even swallow her saliva and had to spit it out frequently. Since she was too weak to get up each time, Grandpa and Sameer uncle placed two bowls and rolls of tissue paper beside her bed. On top of that, Grandma was suffering from severe coughing, adding to the challenge of her condition.

The sight of her cough-filled saliva was horrifying. At this point, Grandma was also losing consciousness frequently. I watched her shiver under the blanket, her expression vacant and her mouth filled with saliva, which prevented her from speaking. She would occasionally try to express how she was feeling, but often she lay in bed with her eyes open, seemingly unaware of who was visiting. She stopped responding to our conversations.

Despite this, Grandpa, Sameer uncle, Shanaya Aunty and Mom continued to talk to her, even if it felt like a one-sided conversation. Grandma couldn't even sit up during her feeding times; she was so weak that she would lie down after just the first glass of liquid food. Grandpa would alternate between encouraging her, crying, and pleading with her to stay upright until she had finished her portion. He even enlisted Sameer uncle's help to scold her, as Grandma seemed to respond more to him.

Sometimes, Mom would visit with wheatgrass juice with me and stay for the feeding session. I saw Grandpa, Sameer uncle and Mom diligently cleaning Grandma's face after she spat out saliva into the bowl. It was an incredibly moving sight, yet it was also a period when our hopes were dwindling, tensions were rising, and smiles had vanished from our faces. Grandpa seemed to be living like a machine, devoid of emotion. I wondered if he felt the absence of Grandma's full presence and whether he would ever be able to communicate with her in the way they once did.

Grandpa's face spoke volumes about his internal struggle, even if he couldn't articulate his feelings. I saw Mom crying in front of Dad, overwhelmed by the distress of seeing both of her parents in such a state—one unresponsive and speechless, the other nearly in tears.

Does cancer affect only one person, or does it impact the entire family? Doesn't it test everyone's patience? The answer is "yes." Abhi and I had promised to lift the spirits of our elders, but despite our best efforts, we couldn't hold back our own tears.

In Mumbai, the entire family was grappling with the impact of cancer. Meanwhile, in Porbandar, Grandma and Grandpa's siblings—Grandma's two brothers and two sisters, along with Grandpa's two sisters—were deeply concerned. Each of them called Grandpa and Sameer uncle every other day to inquire about Grandma's condition. As the caregiving demands on Sameer uncle and Grandpa intensified, they began reaching out to Mom for updates.

Mom provided detailed reports, which only heightened their concern. Although they masked their anxiety over the phone, their messages were filled with wishes for Grandma's speedy recovery and heartfelt prayers.

"Oh God, I have so much love and so many cherished memories with these wonderful grandparents," I prayed fervently. "I want to share my countless life experiences of my studies, school and college with them and dedicate many future awards and rewards to them. Please bring them back together. My heart prayed with all its might, hoping that more prayers would bring better results."

Sameer uncle took on the responsibility of regularly escorting Grandma to her radiation and chemotherapy sessions, often postponing his client meetings to do so. Grandpa was entirely focused on meeting Grandma's food needs, administering her medicines, assisting with toileting, bathing her, and even combing her hair which were thinning every day. Mom, me and Abhi made frequent visits to Grandma's home with wheatgrass juice, while Shanaya aunty prepared nutritious dishes for Grandpa to give to Grandma. Dad made a variety of juices and prepared sprouts to support Grandma's nutrition.

Meanwhile, Abhi and I prayed fervently and tried to keep the atmosphere as cheerful as possible whenever at Grandma's place.

"Okay, let's start with a joke," Abhi suggested, grinning. "Why did the scarecrow win an award?"

"I don't know, why?" I asked, trying to suppress a laugh.

"Because he was outstanding in his field!" he said, bursting into laughter.

I rolled my eyes playfully. "You're really reaching for the corniness, aren't you?"

"Hey, I'm just trying to plant some positivity here!" he shot back with a wink. "Besides, if we can't laugh now, when can we?"

"True, but if you tell one more bad joke, I might have to start praying for your comedy skills!" I teased.

The elders would deliberately laugh out loud, hiding their own tears each time we kids tried to cheer them up just to acknowledge our efforts.

It felt as though every family member was affected by cancer, each fighting their own battle. The siblings of Grandma and Grandpa were a source of immense support and motivation, and everyone had a crucial role to play in this collective effort.

Somehow, we managed to get through four chemotherapy and the respective radiation sessions regularly. However, when it was time for the fifth session, the doctor checked Grandma's white blood cell count to assess her readiness. After reviewing the results, he said with concern, "Her WBC count has dropped significantly. I'm afraid we can't proceed with the chemotherapy today."

"But we've come all this way," Sameer uncle said anxiously. "What do we do now?"

The doctor replied, "I'm going to administer an injection to help boost her count, but we'll need to postpone the chemotherapy. Her body isn't ready for it."

"Will this delay affect her recovery?" Sameer uncle asked, worriedly.

The doctor reassured us, "The side effects of chemotherapy and radiation will eventually subside once the treatments are completed. However, due to Kaishma's age and the dangerously low white blood cell count, we need to be cautious. The sessions will be delayed until her counts improve."

Despite his reassurances, the ongoing delays and the toll they were taking on Grandma's health were deeply concerning.

Chapter 7 End of the Treatment Regimen

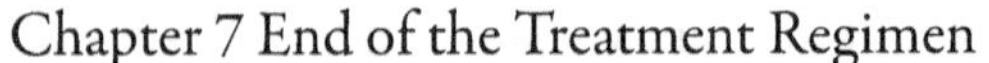

The fifth chemotherapy session was delayed by two days. Once administered, the chemo made Grandma feel even weaker. After each session, she would collapse onto the bed, barely able to move. At times, she would shiver despite the room being warm. When we asked her what was wrong, she wouldn't respond, seeming to be completely out of touch with her surroundings. We were concerned whether she could even hear us.

Then came the final, sixth chemotherapy session. We prayed earnestly that this session would go smoothly and bring some relief once it was over. Although her white blood cell count was still low, this time, there was less concern given the familiar routine. The doctors administered another WBC-boosting injection and gave the final chemotherapy two days later.

The radiation treatment also concluded with the 28th session in the first week of January 2024. As the treatments ended, a visible sense of relief and joy spread across Grandma and Grandpa's faces. It felt like a celebration of their personal Independence Day.

"Is it too early for a victory dance?" Grandpa joked, wiggling his eyebrows.

"I think we've earned one!" Grandma replied, her eyes sparkling, even though she couldn't speak much. Her smile said it all.

"Just promise not to break anything, okay?" I teased, laughing.

Grandpa chuckled, "I'm not that fragile yet! Let's just say I'm a classic—still in good shape!"

The air was filled with a lightness that had been missing for so long. We could see smiles returning, and there was laughter where there had been silence.

"Remember when we thought we'd never get through this?" I said, looking at them both.

Grandma managed a small, triumphant laugh, while Grandpa nodded vigorously. "And here we are, ready to take on the world again!"

With it being New Year's, the atmosphere was already filled with a sense of hope and renewal, making the moment even more special and poignant.

"Let's make this year the best one yet!" I declared, raising an imaginary glass.

"To new beginnings!" Grandpa exclaimed, and Grandma beamed, her joy infectious.

It felt like half the battle had been won. The doctor had assured us, "Once the sessions are over, Grandma's recovery will begin, and her health will improve. At least she won't need to visit the hospital anymore."

"What a relief!" Sameer uncle exclaimed. "It's such a weight off our shoulders."

However, this sense of relief quickly faded. As days passed, we hoped for a swift recovery, expecting Grandma's health to bounce back and for her to regain weight soon. But when we weighed her, the reality hit hard. Dad's voice wavered as he said, "Mom's weight has dropped to just 50 kg. I thought we'd see improvement by now."

Mom sighed deeply. "I guess the path to recovery is going to be longer than we anticipated."

We all faced the sobering truth together: the road to recovery was still a long one. The doctors now said their role was complete. "From here on," they explained, "it's up to the family and the patient's willpower to see this through." The artificial feeding tube remained in place, and while the coughing had lessened, Grandma still had to manage the constant need to spit out saliva.

Chapter 8 The Radiant Aunt and celebration times

Then came my cheerful and endlessly optimistic Jamna Fai. In Gujarati, dad's sister is called "Fai". Though she is my mom's fai, i.e. my Grandpa's elder sister, me and Abhi also call her fai. Despite being around 83 years old, she doesn't show her age in the slightest. Jamna Fai is incredibly talkative, chatting away for hours on end without needing much from anyone in return. Her presence is a breath of fresh air, filling the room with positive energy.

"Look at you, all grown up!" she would say with a twinkle in her eye, addressing anyone who entered the room. "I remember when you were just a little squirt running around here."

It was as if Grandpa felt that his mother had returned; his face clearly reflected this emotion. "It feels like I've got Ma back," he confided with a smile, eyes misty.

With Jamna Fai able to sit for long hours and converse with Grandma—albeit one-sided—Grandpa was able to focus more on preparing food for Grandma. "Don't worry about Grandma," Jamna Fai would say cheerfully, "just make sure she's eating well. I'll keep her company."

During this time, we celebrated Grandma and Grandpa's 52nd wedding anniversary with Jamna Fai present. As we gathered around the table, stories were shared, laughter echoed, and memories were rekindled. The fragrance of fifty-two years of love and commitment spread in the air, a testament to the enduring bond between Grandma and Grandpa. She recited some Sanskrit prayers for her younger brother and sister-in-law, which deeply moved Grandpa. Grandpa, who rarely spoke, was clearly moved by the intensity of Jamna Fai's invocation. Tradition and affection were weighed down by her voice, which was a comforting salve. "May your life be blessed with peace and joy," she intoned softly, her voice full of warmth. Grandpa's eyes welled up as he listened. A lifetime of shared experiences, joys, and sorrows flashed before his eyes. In that moment, the passage of time seemed insignificant. He was grateful for the love and support of his family, especially his dear sister. "Thank you, Sister," he managed to say, his voice choked with emotion.

While the occasion was a time of celebration, there was an underlying worry among us all. Gradually, Grandpa, Fai, Mom, and Sameer uncle encouraged Grandma to swallow, even if just saliva, but she struggled with this.

"Ganga, just try to swallow a little bit," Grandpa would gently coax. "You can do it, dear."

Jamna Fai added, "Come on, Ganga, you've got this. Just a little bit at a time."

Now gradually, Grandma remained conscious and began taking the bowl herself, spitting out saliva and cleaning her mouth with a tissue. "Look at her!" Jamna Fai exclaimed, clapping her hands in delight. "She's really trying!"

The therapy sessions, though challenging, had begun to bear fruit. Whether it was Jamna Fai's presence or the culmination of the sessions, we were heartened to see these small signs of improvement.

Eventually, after 3 weeks the day came for Jamna Fai to leave. Although we were reluctant to see her go, she had other commitments.

"We'll miss you so much, Fai," Mom said with a heavy heart.

"Oh, don't you worry," Jamna Fai replied with her usual cheerfulness. "I'll be back soon. You take care of yourselves, okay?"

With heavy hearts, we said our farewells, grateful for the time she spent with us and the hope she brought. "Safe travels, Fai," Grandpa said, holding her hand tightly. "We'll be waiting for your return."

Despite nearly two months of treatment, the feeding tube was still in place, and Ganga couldn't manage to swallow saliva. Grandpa and Sameer uncle tried giving her spoonful of water to drink with mouth, but grandma found even this uncomfortable and difficult to swallow. Her original esophagus was completely dry.

Then Sameer uncle came up with a new idea: he brought some honey-filled candy for Grandma to keep in her mouth and savor slowly. Grandma responded positively to this, and she began to retain the candy in her mouth instead of spitting it out. After a week of this progress, Sameer uncle introduced ice cream. Grandma was thrilled at the prospect of eating it.

Ice cream played a pivotal role in Grandma's recovery. If my family were to honor those who contributed to her health, ice cream would undoubtedly be a key figure. By this time, Grandma could speak a little, though her conversations were still limited.

"This is the best part of the day," Grandma would say with a faint smile as she enjoyed her ice cream. "It's like a little bit of heaven."

The cold ice cream seemed to provide her with soothing relief, almost as if it were a healing balm. "It feels so nice and cold," she'd remark, her eyes closing in contentment. "I think it's really helping."

Sameer uncle would often add, "I'm so glad you're enjoying it, Mom. It's the little things that make a difference, right?"

Grandma would nod, her expression one of deep satisfaction. "Yes, it really does feel like it's helping. Thank you for bringing it to me."

The comforting effect of the ice cream was clear; it wasn't just a treat, but a crucial part of her healing process.

Encouraged by this, Sameer uncle and Grandpa gradually started giving grandma small amounts of solid food to eat by mouth. After a couple of practice sessions, Grandpa stopped blending the food and began serving complete meals. However, now the obstacle was the feeding tube, which made swallowing difficult. Though the cancerous tumor had completely melted away, the tube was hindering grandma's ability to eat.

Faced with this challenge, Grandpa and Sameer uncle decided to remove the feeding tube. On March 7th, a day of celebration, Grandma was finally freed from it, marking a significant milestone in her recovery.

Then, for the first time, she began speaking fluently. Once she started, there was no stopping her.

"You know what?" Ganga said to all of us, her voice filled with emotion. "I thought that feeding tube was going to be with me for the rest of my life. It felt like the world had stopped. There was no day or night—just that ugly feeding tube in front of me. I felt so cheated when it was inserted."

Grandpa looked at her, smiling through his tears. "We were all so worried about you, dear. It's amazing to hear you talk like this."

"I'm just so happy to see you well again," Uncle Sameer continued, feeling both relieved and delighted. "You've shown such strength."

His words brought a mix of laughter and tears of joy to all our faces. Grandma couldn't stop expressing her gratitude to everyone.

"Thank you, dear," she said to Grandpa, her voice warm. "And Sameer, you were always so encouraging. I couldn't have done it without all of you."

She turned to Mom and Shanaya Aunty, saying, "You've been my rock. I appreciate everything you've done."

Dad, with a proud smile, said, "You've made so much progress. We're all so proud of you."

Grandma eagerly made video calls to all her relatives at Porbandar. "Look at me now!" she exclaimed to one of them. "I'm feeling so much better, and it's all thanks to you for your prayers and support."

She shared the news of her improved health with them personally. "I wanted to let you know how much your encouragement meant to me. Look at how far we've come!"

Two days later, the final PET scan report arrived. The crucial line in the report read, "No definite evidence of metabolically active lesion to suggest metastatic/residual disease. Esophageal lesion has resolved. Complete metabolic response." By then, we were all well-informed enough to understand the significance of this finding. Confirming it with the doctor was merely a formality.

The next day, Sameer uncle happily took the report to the doctor. The report stated that there were no signs of cancer in the esophagus, but the doctor wanted to examine Grandma personally. Three days later, Sameer uncle took Grandma to doctor with equal joy. This time, the doctor was astonished and thrilled by the results of his treatment. He confirmed that Grandma had made a full recovery and assured us that there was no need to worry anymore.

"Oh my God, bless him," we all exclaimed in gratitude.

A month later, we gathered once more, this time to enjoy each other's company as a happy family. The conversation had shifted from Grandma's health to a new and exciting topic: the book I planned to write in honor of her full recovery. It would be a tribute to Grandma's truly inspiring journey—a testament not just to battle illness but to courage, patience, love, care, and most importantly, hope.

"Dedicated to my beautiful grandmother!" I said. "Best live, long live."

Epilogue:

Six months after the PET scan results, Grandma has fully regained her hair that had been lost during chemotherapy. She has also regained her weight, though not to her previous level, but to a healthy and respectable amount.

We celebrated my birthday and the entire family including grandpa and grandma gathered for the party. Grandpa and Grandma visited Porbandar, and their siblings were coming over almost every day to see Grandma personally. Grandma was now talking non-stop and Grandpa no longer tried to hold her back.

Sameer Uncle had given a lengthy list of instructions for Grandma and Grandpa to follow while in Porbandar, but it was clear that they had little intention of sticking to his advice! Poor Sameer uncle never gets tired of handling these two kiddos! They are reliving their childhood and youth once again.

And the life continues........